The Duke Who Outlawed Jelly Beans

AND OTHER STORIES

By Johnny Valentine
Illustrated by Lynette Schmidt

ALYSON WONDERLAND

To Raymond Macdonald Alden, whose stories stirred
a sense of wonder in me as a child and whose
"Knights of the Silver Shield" served as inspiration
for "The Eaglerider" in this book.
—J.V.

In memory of Tim Patton, one of my drawing students,
and his family, Dr. Michael Q. Patton and Dr. Jeanne Campbell
in particular, because they brought him, themselves,
and so much else into my life.
—L.S.

TEXT © 1991 BY JOHNNY VALENTINE.
ARTWORK © 1991 BY LYNETTE SCHMIDT.
ALL RIGHTS RESERVED.

MANUFACTURED IN CHINA.

THIS BOOK IS PUBLISHED BY ALYSON WONDERLAND,
AN IMPRINT OF ALYSON PUBLICATIONS,
P.O. BOX 4371, LOS ANGELES, CALIFORNIA 90078-4371.
DISTRIBUTION IN THE UNITED KINGDOM BY TURNAROUND PUBLISHER SERVICES LTD.,
UNIT 3, OLYMPIA TRADING ESTATE, COBURG ROAD, WOOD GREEN,
LONDON N22 6TZ ENGLAND.

FIRST EDITION (HARDCOVER): OCTOBER 1991
(PUBLISHED WITH ISBN 1-55583-199-0.)
FIRST PAPERBACK EDITION: JULY 1993
(PUBLISHED WITH ISBN 1-55583-219-9.)
SECOND EDITION: MAY 2004

04 05 06 07 08 ❖ 10 9 8 7 6 5 4 3 2 1

ISBN 1-55583-847-2

The Frog Prince

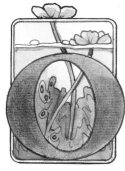

nce upon a time, in a small village in a faraway kingdom, a boy named Nicholas lived with his father. Nicholas's father had a friend named Karl, who wore a bushy black beard and who often carried Nicholas around the yard on his shoulders. But Nicholas had no friends his own age, so many days he played by himself.

One day he sat by the well outside his house. He threw in a small round pebble and counted fast to see how high he could get before it struck the water.

"One-two-three-four-five-six—" counted Nicholas quickly, then he heard *ker-plunk*.

He threw in another pebble. "One-two-three-four-five-six-seven—"

But this time, instead of a *ker-plunk*, a voice hollered up: "Hey, stop that! You could hurt somebody!"

Nicholas peered into the dark well. "Who's down there?"

"Me," answered the voice. A moment later, a big frog hopped up and sat beside him. "That second pebble practically hit me!"

"I didn't know frogs could talk," said Nicholas.

"They can't." The frog looked up at Nicholas with its bright green eyes. "But I'm not a frog. I'm a prince."

"Oh," said Nicholas. That sounded impossible. But a talking frog was impossible too. He turned to the frog.

"I suppose you're going to ask me to kiss you." He had read about something like that in a fairy tale. "Well, forget it. I won't do it."

The frog looked up. "That's *exactly* what I was going to ask. And you've *got* to do it. That's the only way I can turn back into a prince!"

"I won't," declared Nicholas.

"You've *got* to," pleaded the frog.

"I don't believe you're really a prince," replied Nicholas.

"I'll prove it," offered the frog. "Ask me

something. Ask me anything a prince would know."

"What's three plus seven?" asked Nicholas. He wasn't entirely sure, but he thought he'd recognize a wrong answer if he heard it.

"Princes don't do *arithmetic,*" groaned the frog. "We have bookkeepers for that. Ask me something else."

"How do you spell 'dog'?" asked Nicholas.

"Oh, honestly," complained the frog. "Princes don't *spell*. That's why we have scribes."

"Well, then, I give up," announced Nicholas. This game bored him. He changed the subject to something more interesting. "What's your favorite dessert, Frog?" he asked.

"Easy," replied the frog. "Chocolate ice cream. Now kiss me."

"That wasn't *that* kind of question," protested Nicholas. Then he paused. A frog wouldn't like chocolate ice cream…but a prince might.

"OK," he finally agreed. He leaned over, wrinkled his nose, and, as lightly and quickly as he could, he kissed the top of the frog's head.

No sooner had he done so than something wonderful happened. Instantly the frog turned into a boy the same age as Nicholas. Dressed in a fine purple robe with gold lace, the boy wore a green cloak over his shoulders, attached in front by a silver medallion.

"Thank you," said the prince graciously. "Being a frog is awful! Now, for one hour, we can play together! I've never played with another boy before!"

"What do you mean?" asked Nicholas.

"My mother and father are the king and queen. Sometimes they're nice to me and give me gifts. I have a beautiful pony and all kinds of toys. But they don't think I should play with other children. Most days they have no time for me, and sometimes they're cruel. This morning I spilled my juice at breakfast. Do you know how they punished me? They gave me to the wizard to use for his experiments!"

"Did the wizard turn you into a frog?"

"Yes. But you broke the spell for one hour. After that hour, I'll turn back into a frog, and I'll have to hop back to the castle dungeon so the wizard can remove the spell."

A tear glistened in the prince's eye. "I've been through this before," he explained. "I'm afraid that one day I'll return and the wizard will be gone. He changes the spell each time, so without him, I'd be a frog forever!"

For an hour, Nicholas and the prince played. Nicholas showed the prince his secret cave by the river. They boys threw pine cones into the water and watched them vanish downstream. And then, without warning, Nicholas heard a *pop!* and where the prince had been standing a moment ago, the frog now crouched.

"I have to go back," sighed the frog. "I wish I could stay, but I have no choice."

"I'll come with you," Nicholas declared. As they walked to the castle, Nicholas thought how much happier the prince would be if he could stay and they could play together. The prince could even live with Nicholas's family. But Nicholas had no idea how to break the spell.

"It's getting dark," said Nicholas as they walked along. "Let's hurry." He reached down and picked up the frog that hopped next to him.

"Hey, wait up!" called a voice from

behind. Another frog hopped up the road after him. "I just stepped behind the bushes to zap a fly, and when I came back, you were way ahead."

Nicholas studied the frog in his hand. This frog's head was shaped differently. The frog on the ground was the real prince!

Now Nicholas had an idea. "When we reach the castle," he whispered to the frog-prince, "don't go inside."

And so, after they crossed the moat and crept to the dungeon window, the frog-prince stayed close to Nicholas. They peeked through the iron grating on the window. Inside, the wizard hovered over a bubbling flask. Gently Nicholas tossed the real frog through the window.

"So, my little prince, you've come back!" exclaimed the wizard. "And a good thing too. The king and queen would be quite annoyed if I lost you. Though they probably wouldn't notice for a few weeks."

Saying that, he scooped the frog off the floor and set it on the table. He raised his hands, then rapidly chanted:

"Fingers, toes, eyes, and thumb,
Green frog now a prince become!"
Nothing happened. The wizard wrinkled his brow. The frog tried to hop away, but the wizard grabbed it and repeated the chant:

"Fingers, toes, eyes, and thumb,
Green frog now a prince become!"
Still nothing happened. The third time the wizard frantically yelled:

"Fingers, toes, eyes, and thumb,
Green frog now a prince become!"
But the frog just sat there. Angrily the wizard snatched it up and peered into its eyes. "You're not the prince!" he suddenly bellowed. In a fit of rage, he hurled his flask against the wall.

"We've seen enough. Let's go," whispered

Nicholas. They stole back across the moat.

"The spell seems pretty easy," said Nicholas, once they were clear of the castle. "All I have to say is—what was it?

Fingers, toes, nose and thumb
Green frog now a prince become—"

As soon as he uttered the last word, the frog disappeared and the prince again stood next to Nicholas. He smiled radiantly. "Thank you!" he exclaimed. "I am free of the wizard." Then he frowned. "But I still have to go home, and my parents will give me back to him soon. I know they will."

"You don't have to go back," said Nicholas. "You can come with me. My father and his friend Karl have always said they'd like another son. You'd be welcome in our family, and they would never be cruel to you."

"They wouldn't be the same as real parents," protested the prince.

"Sure they would," said Nicholas. "My dad adopted *me*, and he's pretty real. He could adopt you too."

The prince shuddered at the thought of going back to the castle, so he agreed.

Nicholas was right. When they got home, Nicholas told what had happened. His father and Karl agreed that certainly the prince should become a part of the family. "But one father isn't enough for two boys," said Karl. "Perhaps I'd better move in too, to keep you out of mischief." His eyes twinkled as he looked at Nicholas's father.

"I think that would be a good idea," said Nicholas's father, and he smiled back.

"We need to give you a name," said Karl. "We can't call you 'prince' all the time."

"When I was little, my favorite uncle was named Jesse," said the prince. "I like that name. You can call me that." And they did.

In the years that followed, Nicholas and Jesse and their two fathers had many happy times together. At first Jesse was shy, but only because he had never played with other kids before.

I'm glad that I grew up with a father who loves me, thought Nicholas. Now that Karl had moved in, Nicholas and Jesse both had two wonderful fathers. Nothing could be better than that.

It so happened that Jesse and Karl both had dark hair and dimples. As the years went by, many people assumed Karl had always been Jesse's father. Sometimes Jesse or Karl patiently explained what had really happened. Other times they didn't bother.

But there was one thing that no one—not even the four members of the family—could ever explain. Where, they all wondered, had Jesse gotten his vivid green eyes?

The Eaglerider

In one of the many homes in the village, a girl named Scarlett lived with her mother.

As a small girl, Scarlett spent many afternoons watching the Eagleriders of the kingdom as they soared through the sky. It was their job to watch for invading dragons from the rocky hills to the north.

She had befriended two of the Eagleriders, boys who had been chosen because they were small enough to ride an eagle yet brave enough that if a dragon appeared, they would not run away but would fly directly to the Great Tower and report the danger. After two years the boys would grow too heavy to ride, and new Eagleriders would replace them.

Many, many years had passed since anyone had seen a dragon in the kingdom. But they never stopped watching. "The dragons stay away because they know we are watching," the king told the villagers. "We must always have Eagleriders."

Scarlett wanted to be an Eaglerider too. But only boys were accepted. It had been that way for many years. Although no one remembered the reason, the Eaglemaster explained that, "We don't know if girls can do the job, and we must take no chances."

His words left Scarlett disappointed and angry.

One day Scarlett told her mother about her dream of becoming an Eaglerider. "Perhaps we can do something," her mother said. And she told Scarlett a story.

"Many years ago," Scarlett's mother began, "when I was a young woman, I fell in love for the first time. But I fell in love with another woman, and in my country, many people did not like that. Sometimes when we traveled, we couldn't find a place to stay. So I cut my hair short and dressed like a man. We traveled south to the land of elves. We went north and saw the dragons. No one ever guessed my secret.

"If you like," she continued, "we can cut your hair and dress you like a boy. I know you can be the best Eaglerider of all!"

The next day, Scarlett's mother cut her long hair, then made her a shirt and trousers.

Scarlett went to the Eaglemaster. "My name is Red," she announced, "and I want

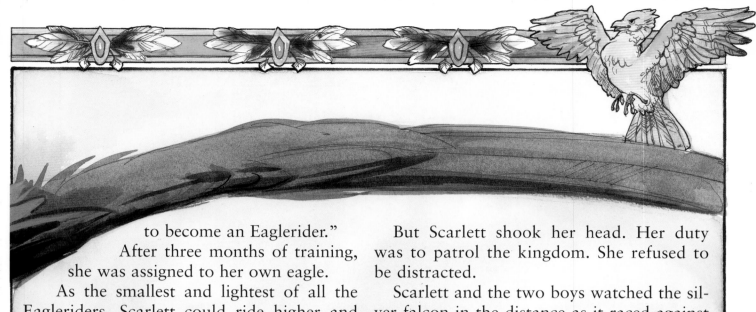

to become an Eaglerider."

After three months of training, she was assigned to her own eagle.

As the smallest and lightest of all the Eagleriders, Scarlett could ride higher and faster than the others. In races, she circled the castle turret twice before some of the boys had circled it the first time.

Once each week, Scarlett patrolled the kingdom with two other Eagleriders. They scanned the horizon for the telltale green of dragon smoke. If they saw it, one rider was to report immediately to the Great Tower, while the other two watched carefully to see which way the dragons were flying.

Some boys complained that their job was boring because they never saw any dragons. But Scarlett never complained. Each week she looked for ways to fly better than before.

As Scarlett and Jason and Joshua patrolled the kingdom one day, another Eaglerider flew up to her. "Red!" he cried. "Jason! Joshua! A silver falcon has appeared and is bragging that she is faster than all of us. Come race. We'll show her!"

But Scarlett shook her head. Her duty was to patrol the kingdom. She refused to be distracted.

Scarlett and the two boys watched the silver falcon in the distance as it raced against her friends. One by one, the other Eagleriders were defeated.

Soon Ethelbert flew over. "We're losing!" he cried. "We can't let the falcon think she's better than any of us. You're the three fastest Eagleriders in the kingdom. Come help!"

"We can't," Scarlett answered sorrowfully. "We're on patrol. Sure, we could beat that falcon, but the villagers trust us to stay on duty."

"Wait, Red," interrupted Joshua. "This'll just take a few minutes." Before anyone could say a word, he flew off.

Scarlett and Jason watched as Joshua soared up to the falcon. They circled once to begin the race.

And then they were off! Joshua took the lead, but the silver falcon closed quickly from behind. Then Scarlett shook her head. *My job is to watch for dragons,* she thought, angry with herself. *I can't let this distract me.* She searched the horizon for green smoke. As

always, however, the sky was clear.

"Red!" exclaimed Jason, "Joshua lost! He had the lead, but then he got tired, and the silver falcon finished first. Now Joshua looks too tired to fly any more."

Ethelbert had been flying with Scarlett and Jason. Now he pleaded with the two Eagleriders.

"You're our last hope! Please go race. It'll just take a few minutes, and anyone who can defeat the silver falcon will be a hero!"

"I can defeat that silly bird," declared Jason. And off he flew.

Once again, Scarlett vowed not to let the race distract her. But Ethelbert announced everything that happened.

"The falcon started ahead, but now Jason is catching up," Ethelbert told her excitedly. "Now Jason is ahead. But he turned too wide. They're even. Now Jason is getting tired… Oh, no! The silver falcon won again." He turned to Scarlett. "Please come race. You know there won't be any dragons. In just a few minutes, you can become a hero. If you refuse to race, everyone will think you're afraid."

A tear filled Scarlett's eye. Everyone knew she was the fastest Eaglerider, and they'd be angry if she didn't race. They might even call her names. But she had vowed to do her job. The villagers had trusted her, and she would not let them down just to show off her speed.

With her gloved hand, she brushed the tear from her eye, and blinked. But her vision was still just a bit hazy. She blinked again. No, her vision wasn't hazy. Her vision was clear. *The haziness was smoke on the horizon. Green smoke.* Dragons were on the way!

But what should she do? Both her patrol partners were too tired to help. "Stay here," she commanded Ethelbert, pointing to the smoke. "Watch the dragons. Keep track of which way they go." And faster than any Eaglerider had ever flown, she raced to the Great Tower.

Within minutes, the bugler sounded the alarm, and everyone in the kingdom turned out to defend their land. Archers took their places in the towers. Knights on white horses lined up at the gate. Giant slings whose projectiles could pierce even a dragon's leather were loaded and pulled back.

The dragons flew closer. In the lead was a winged green creature with teeth as long as its horns. Behind it, the spiked head of a red dragon was barely visible behind the cloud of smoke that billowed from its mouth. Biggest

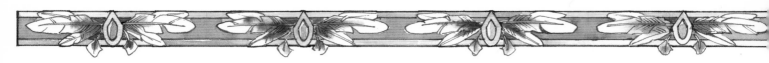

of all was a monster with gold scales and a crimson crest, and sharp talons jutting from its wings.

But when they saw the well-armed villagers, they knew they had lost the advantage of surprise. They could never win. With a giant sweeping motion, the green dragon in front turned aside. Soon the entire invading army had circled around and retreated north.

Suddenly a burst of steam hissed from the silver falcon. As the Eagleriders watched, it turned into a dragon and winged after the others.

"The silver falcon was a dragon in disguise!" exclaimed Jason. "It must have been sent here to distract us while the others attacked!"

Soon word had spread that Red the Eaglerider had saved the kingdom from the dragons. The king declared a national holiday and prepared a ceremony at which Scarlett would be declared a national hero.

To show what a special day it was, the chimes rang at the old stone church. It was the first time anyone could remember hearing the chimes. The king announced that he would present Scarlett with a medal, embossed with the silver shield of the village. Scarlett walked proudly onto the stage.

"Speech! Speech!" the villagers cried. Scarlett thought a moment. "OK," she decided, "I'll give them a speech." She stepped forward. "Thank you for honoring me," she said. "But I think you should know that because of a silly rule, I might not have been in the sky to see the dragons. I'm not a boy named Red—I am a girl named Scarlett!"

The king gasped and pulled back the very hand with which he had held out the medal. "Perhaps we can't give you this medal after all—" he began.

But before he could finish, the queen stepped forward. The queen had not appeared in public for many years, and few people remembered what a strong voice she had.

"We cannot give you just one medal," the queen declared. "You have earned two medals. One for saving the kingdom, and another because you did something much harder. You refused to let prejudice stop you from doing what you wanted. We are all indebted to you."

The crowd roared. Some people were angry, but most were cheering. A small girl ran onto the stage and grabbed Scarlett. "I want to be an Eaglerider too," she said eagerly. "How did you do it?"

"Quiet, please!" called out the queen. "We were wrong to think that only boys could be Eagleriders. From this day on, any child who can pass the test may become an Eaglerider, and our kingdom shall be safer because of it."

Within just a few years, many girls as well as boys became Eagleriders. They took pride in doing the job well. And they were especially proud that their new Eaglemaster was Scarlett, who had been the greatest Eaglerider of them all.

Dragon Sense

One of Scarlett's friends was a boy named Peter. He lived with his mother, who was a bookkeeper, and his mother's friend Daniela, who was a sorcerer.

"How could a bookkeeper and a sorcerer fall in love?" people sometimes asked. "They're so different!" But Peter never found it odd. His family needed his mother's down-to-earth way of looking at things. His mother made sure that dinner got cooked every night, though Peter and Daniela helped.

Yet the family wouldn't have been the same without Daniela to add excitement. One time she transformed Peter's dog, Oscar, into a winged horse for a day. Peter straddled Oscar's back and flew all the way to Wizard's Peak, the mountain shaped like a wizard's face.

Another time one of Daniela's spells went haywire, and a hippopotamus materialized in the family's small living room. Daniela didn't figure out how to reverse the spell for two days. Everyone laughed about it now, but it wasn't funny at the time. It had been pretty smelly.

Unfortunately, Daniela's magic wasn't strong enough to keep the family from being poor. Finding a good job wasn't easy for a lesbian sorcerer—and her magic couldn't pay the rent.

One day the landlord knocked at the door. "I'm here for the rent money," he hollered.

"Oh, no," moaned Peter's mother. "I don't have any money. I wish I knew what to do."

"I'll go get Daniela," Peter offered. "She can change him into a hippopotamus." Before his mother could reply, he ran down the stone steps that led deep into Daniela's workshop. "Daniela," he cried, "you've got to help Mother!" He told her about the angry landlord.

"I can't change the landlord into a hippopotamus," laughed Daniela. "Even if we

don't like him, that would be wrong. But I'll go upstairs and see if I can help." She hurried off, leaving Peter alone in the dark room.

He glanced around. Glass bottles lined the shelves of one wall. On the table a jar bubbled with a pink liquid that smelled like hot chocolate and turpentine mixed together. He knew better than to taste it. Against the other wall stood a huge oak case filled with books. Peter loved to read, so he gently brushed aside the cobwebs and removed the biggest volume.

Soon Peter was immersed in a story of hidden treasure. "The prince locked his wealth in the castle," he read. "Diamonds and emeralds, silver and jewelry, and coins the color of gold. One day the prince set out to slay a dragon. Instead, the dragon ate him, and the treasure still lies in the castle. But the location of the castle has been lost to memory."

Above the writing was a picture of the castle. In the distance behind it loomed a familiar mountain. Peter recognized the mountain—it was Wizard's Peak. But the stone profile was backward! Instead of looking to the right, it looked to the left!

Peter was perplexed. How could a mountain turn around? Then he figured it out. If you looked at Wizard's Peak from the other side, the face would be reversed. The castle was on the other side of the mountain! And the castle held the prince's lost treasure.

"We got rid of the landlord for now," Daniela told Peter when he went upstairs. "But he'll be back next week. I don't know how much longer we can put him off."

"Well, I've decided to go for a long walk," Peter told his mother and Daniela. He packed a few clothes into a knapsack. His mother fixed some sandwiches, and Daniela gave him a large flask of water. Then Peter started out the door.

In just a few minutes, Peter reached the road to the mountain. It stretched ahead like a long brown ribbon, going up one hill, down another, growing narrower and narrower in the distance. *At last,* thought Peter, *just like the people in my books,* I *am going to have some adventures!*

By sunset he had walked many miles. His every muscle ached. As Peter prepared his bed under a tree, an old man walked up the path from behind. Peter jumped with surprise. No one had been there a moment before.

"What brings a boy like you to this land?" the man asked.

"I have learned of hidden treasure, and I'm setting off to find it," Peter answered truthfully.

"And where is this treasure?"

"I'm sorry, but that must be my secret," answered Peter. He didn't want anyone to find the treasure before him. But he didn't want to sound rude either, so he added, "Would you like part of my sandwich?" He turned and reached into his knapsack.

But when he looked back, the old man was gone. In his place stood a great dragon with green scales and eyes so red that a fire seemed to burn within. Peter had read about dragons that could take other forms, but he had never seen one. Dragons could breathe fire too. What if this dragon was hungry? Too hungry for just a sandwich?

But the dragon merely snorted. Then, with a quick flap of its wings, it soared up and disappeared into the night sky.

The next morning, Peter resumed his journey. He reached the mountain, and once he crossed it, he saw the castle just as it had looked in Daniela's book. On his third day of walking, Peter finally reached the castle. It was surrounded by a deep moat and by a thick brier patch that grew around the moat.

The wood of the old drawbridge had been eaten by worms. It looked dangerous. If it crumbled under his weight, he'd tumble into the moat far below. He peered down. A crocodile glared back at him from the moat and snapped its teeth.

Carefully, Peter touched the toe of one shoe to the drawbridge, and leaned back as he put his foot down. The bridge creaked but did not collapse. Slowly he put his weight down and began to cross.

But halfway across the bridge, Peter heard a rustling overhead, like a giant oak tree shaking its leaves. He searched the sky. The sound had come not from a tree, but from a dragon above. The beast soared down toward the castle. As it landed on the far side of the moat, Peter ran the rest of the way across the bridge and into the castle.

The dragon had followed him! From high in the sky, beyond human sight, the dragon, with its keen vision, had followed him to the treasure! Peter slammed the iron gate behind him, but he could see the dragon running across the drawbridge. With a gush of fire, the dragon melted the gate, and then it squeezed through the door.

Peter ran down the great hall, flung open a door, and rushed through. But the room was only a closet, filled with old wooden beams. He was trapped.

The dragon, however, had lost interest in Peter. It marched straight to the treasury.

After Peter heard the dragon pass, he peeked cautiously out from the closet. The great hall was empty. By following the noise of the dragon's heavy breathing, Peter traced it to the treasury.

And then he gasped in astonishment.

Treasure filled the room. Precious stones sparkled as if kissed by the beams of sunlight that streamed through a small window. Rings and bracelets and necklaces covered the shelves. And scattered all around the room were small coins the color of tarnished gold. Peter examined one and smiled. The coin was just a penny! He had read about pennies in one of his books. They looked like gold, but they were worthless. A single emerald was worth more than all the pennies in this room.

The dragon had noticed Peter by now, but it ignored him. The beast hastily scooped things into a large bag. Precious stones and jewelry and pennies—whatever its claws touched—went into the bag.

After all his travel, Peter ached to think that he would go home empty-handed. Then an idea occurred to him.

"Pennies!" he cried out as enthusiastically as he could. "Pennies! With just a few of these I will be rich forever!"

The dragon looked at him. It didn't stop filling the bag, but a tuft of smoke escaped from one nostril.

"Pennies!" cried Peter again. "I never expected all this. I only expected to find diamonds and rubies and silver and gold." He picked up a few of the pennies.

The dragon stopped its task and glowered at Peter. "This is *my* treasure!" bellowed the great reptile. "Don't you dare touch it. Put those pennies back!"

"I led you to this treasure," said Peter. "Don't you think I deserve the best part of it? Please, Dragon."

Instead of answering, the dragon shot a small flame at Peter.

"Oh, spare my life," Peter pleaded, falling to his knees. "I'll even let you have these pennies back."

"You'll do more than that," the dragon snarled. It emptied the bag onto the floor. "I'm not going to carry these silly jewels back with me when I can fill my bag with valuable pennies. Help me. But if you put a single jewel in the bag, *I will barbecue you right here!*"

"Oh, Dragon, you are so unfair," complained Peter, but secretly he smiled as he loaded the sack with pennies. As soon as it was full, the dragon galloped back down the great hall toward the door.

Cautiously, Peter followed. The dragon squeezed past the melted gate, then started across the drawbridge. Suddenly a loud crack shook the air. With its bag full of pennies, the dragon was too heavy for the old draw-bridge! The great creature shrieked wildly and tried to bat its wings, but already the moat walls were too close. Peter heard a loud splash, then a hiss of steam. He ran to the drawbridge. Only a few bubbles popped on the surface to show where the dragon had sunk.

Peter walked back to the treasury and stuffed his pockets with the prettiest of the gemstones and jewels. He took a wooden beam from the closet and pushed it across the moat, then carefully walked across. The jewels would last him and his mothers for many years. And when they were gone, he knew where to come for more.

The Ogre's Boots

wo mothers lived in the kingdom with their daughter, Little Jenny, and her big brother, Dan. Although she was surrounded by happiness, Little Jenny got tired of always being the smallest. She couldn't reach the apples on the tree, she couldn't reach the handle on the fence gate, and when the family went for a walk, her legs quickly tired from trying to keep up with her mothers and her brother.

"You'll be taller next year," Mother Barbara assured her. "You'll see." But the next year was too far away. Jenny wanted to be bigger now.

One day while Little Jenny and Dan and their mothers shopped in the village, they heard a *thump, thump, thump* in the distance. Soon the sound grew louder: *THUMP, THUMP, THUMP.* Jenny looked up. Coming toward town was a giant ogre. He wore a robe with a long sash, and a golden locket glittered from his neck.

With a few more steps, the ogre reached the village. "Aaargh!" he roared. All the villagers looked up in fear. No one had ever seen such a giant creature before.

"I've come for dinner," bellowed the ogre. He reached down and snatched up the innkeeper, who stood near Jenny. As all the villagers gasped and drew back, the ogre stomped away, the innkeeper in his fist, back to the mountain cave where he lived.

ord quickly spread, and soon everyone in the kingdom knew about the ogre. The king and queen called an emergency council, but no one knew what to do. "Let's hope he's satisfied now and that he won't come back," the king said.

But the ogre wasn't satisfied. A week later, Little Jenny heard the *THUMP, THUMP, THUMP* of his footsteps. The ogre was back!

This time the ogre stopped right next to Jenny and her family. "I'm hungry again!" he announced. He looked around, then down at his feet he spotted Jenny's mother Josie. "Aha! There's a tasty morsel," he roared. Before she could flee, he reached down and snatched up Mother Josie.

"Stop! You can't do that!" yelled Dan. He ran up and punched the ogre's feet.

"What's that, a gnat?" snarled the ogre. "Begone, or I'll crunch you to dust." With a flick of his foot, he knocked Dan away.

"Stop!" cried Little Jenny. She grabbed the smallest of the three toes on the ogre's foot, but he didn't even notice her. He began to walk away.

"Stop!" she cried again. She seized hold of the sash that hung from the ogre's waist, and she clung to it as he strode away.

Again, word quickly spread through the kingdom. "We

must do something this time," proclaimed the queen. "We'll offer a reward to anyone who rids us of the ogre. Whoever can bring me the golden locket he wears around his neck shall have all the gold they can carry."

eanwhile, the ogre had stomped from the village. Little Jenny's whole body shook as she fought to keep her grip on his sash. She knew Mother Barbara and Dan would be frightened for her, but she had to save Mother Josie.

In just 12 steps the ogre reached his cave high in the mountains. Inside, he threw Mother Josie into a cage. "I'll have to

fatten you up for a few days," he told her. "Then it's off to the grill." With that, the ogre lay down for a nap.

As soon as she heard him snoring, Little Jenny crept over to the cage. Mother Josie was horrified to see her. "Little Jenny!" she exclaimed. "What are you doing here? The ogre will hurt you!"

"Don't worry," said Little Jenny. "I'm going to get you out." But the cage was locked, and try as she might, she could not open it.

Little Jenny searched everywhere for the key, but with no success. Finally, she heard a soft voice from a box in the corner. She hurried over. "Is somebody there?" she whispered.

"Yes," answered a voice. "Let us out of this box." She unfastened the clasp on the

box. In a flash, three elves no bigger than Jenny leaped out.

"I'm Herdy," said the first one. "I'm Gerdie," said the second. "And I'm Gelsa," said the third. "The ogre keeps us prisoner here and makes us work for him. Will you help us escape?"

"First we have to free my Mother Josie," said Little Jenny.

"Hmm," said Herdy. "That's going to be tricky. The ogre keeps the key in the locket around his neck. We can't take it without waking him. But if you'll lure him away, perhaps we can saw through the bars of the cage."

"How can I lure him away?" asked Little Jenny.

"You see those boots?" Gerdie pointed at two enormous boots near the sleeping ogre. "Those are magic seven-league boots. The ogre forced us to make them. With those boots, you can walk seven leagues in one step. You can carry things heavier than you ever thought. And you can walk wherever you wish—even on clouds. Put them on."

Little Jenny walked over to the boots. They towered above her! She climbed up the

laces to the top of one boot. As soon as she put her foot inside, the boot shrank to fit her foot perfectly. She did the same with the other, and it shrank too. Just as the elves had promised, these were magic boots!

But no sooner had she put the second boot on than a cuckoo bird popped out of the clock on the wall. "Master, wake up! Master, wake up!" it called. "There's a thief in the cave! There's a thief in the cave!"

The ogre opened his eyes, and Little Jenny dashed to the door. As he spied her, the ogre let out a roar. "Stop!" he demanded. But Little Jenny ran as fast as she could, with the ogre in close pursuit.

Up one mountain they raced and down the other side, through valleys and forests and up another mountain. The ogre could never quite catch up, but Little Jenny couldn't get away. Suddenly the mountain stopped at the edge of a cliff. Little Jenny frantically glanced around. The bottom was so far below that she couldn't step down to it, even in seven-league boots. And the ogre was not far behind!

But just out from the cliff was a cloud.

Little Jenny remembered what the elves had said, and she stepped out onto the cloud. Her boot sank just a little, then it stopped. She stepped onto the next cloud.

The ogre reached the edge of the cliff too, and stepped onto the cloud. But his foot sank through it. With a loud shriek, he plunged earthward. When he finally hit the ground, the trees shook for miles around. The ogre was dead.

Little Jenny stepped carefully back to the cliff and climbed down to the dead ogre. She took the locket from his neck—in case

the elves couldn't get Mother Josie free, she wanted the key. Then she hurried back to the cave.

The bars on the cage had proved too strong for Herdy, Gerdie, and Gelsa, and Mother Josie was still locked inside. Little

Jenny took the key from the locket and freed her mother. Everyone cheered and hugged each other. Then the elves said goodbye and returned to their home.

The journey would have taken many days for Little Jenny and Mother Josie at their usual speed, but Little Jenny still wore the seven-league boots. "Hop on my back, Mother," she said. Since the locket was made of gold, she picked it up as well. Soon they were home again.

Little Jenny knew nothing about the reward offered by the queen. But when she arrived in the village with the locket, everyone knew the ogre was dead. The villagers shouted the news from the rooftops and cheered their new hero.

The queen invited Little Jenny to the castle treasury to claim her reward. "She's so small, she won't be able to carry away much gold," said the king. "Why don't we let the prince do it for her?"

"Don't worry about me," said Little Jenny, who was still wearing her seven-league boots. In a moment, she had gathered up every bit of gold in the treasury, then walked swiftly out of sight.

The king and queen stared at each other with their mouths open. "Put out a call for some new taxes," the king finally said to his clerk.

But before the clerk could move, Little Jenny returned. She set the gold back in place. "I don't really need all this," she said. "I just don't like people thinking that I'm too small to do things for myself. I'll only keep a few pieces—that's enough for my family and me to live very comfortably."

She is much bigger now, but everyone still calls her Little Jenny. They tell the story far and wide about how she saved the village from the ogre.

And once a year, when no one is watching, Little Jenny puts on her seven-league boots and goes for a walk in the clouds, where no one can follow.

The Duke Who Outlawed Jelly Beans

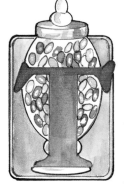

The kingdom was ruled by a king and queen, who one day called all their subjects to hear a proclamation.

"Here ye, hear ye," announced the king from the castle balcony. "The queen and I must go away for many months to visit the Kingdom of Asphodel. While we're away, our nephew, the Grand Duke Archibald, will rule the kingdom." With that, the king and queen climbed into their coach, pulled by six beautiful white horses, and pulled away. Immediately the Grand Duke Archibald strode out on the balcony.

"Hear ye, hear ye," he called out, puffing up his chest. He sounded funny, as if he were holding his nose while he talked.

Among those listening to him was a girl named Anna, who was about the same age as the Grand Duke Archibald. Anna started to giggle.

"Hush," cautioned her mother Marian.

The grand duke continued. "I have a decree to issue." He paused. Then he scratched his head. "My decree is…uh…that everyone must come back tomorrow to hear my next decree."

"That's the stupidest decree I ever heard," declared Anna.

"He probably just couldn't think of anything else," explained Judith, her other mother. "Give him time. He's new at this."

"Doesn't he know how silly he sounds?" asked Anna.

"I think he's pretending to have an

accent," explained Marian. "Some people do that to feel more important."

The next day, everyone returned. The Grand Duke Archibald strutted out on the balcony and puffed up his chest.

"Hear ye, hear ye. I proclaim that too many jelly beans are being eaten. We could have a jelly bean shortage if we're not careful. Henceforth, no one shall eat jelly beans without royal permission. I also proclaim that no one may have royal permission."

Everyone looked at one another. The king and queen had never made such silly pronouncements. One man chuckled loudly.

"Silence!" roared the grand duke. "I am very serious. Anyone found eating jelly beans shall be beheaded. You will all return in one week for my next proclamation."

No one chuckled now. Silently, everyone walked back to their homes. Many shook their heads in dismay as they walked. But no one ate a single jelly bean.

A week later, as promised, the Grand Duke Archibald stepped out on the balcony to issue his next decree:

"Hear ye, hear ye. Today I proclaim that too many children are being impertinent to their parents. Henceforth, no children shall be allowed to read books that have not received the royal seal of approval! Anyone who disobeys shall lose their head."

"He's nuts!" declared Anna.

"I'm afraid that doesn't matter," said Marian. "Until the king and queen return, his word is the law." When they got home, Marian and Judith gathered up Anna's books and sent them to the castle for approval.

"What can I do without my books?" wondered Anna. "I'll be bored!"

"There are other ways to amuse yourself," said Marian. "Why don't you play make-believe?"

So Anna climbed onto the kitchen table. She puffed up her chest. With her left hand she pinched her nose shut, then she announced, "Hear ye, hear ye. I proclaim that anybody who talks like this should have his nose cut off."

"That's very funny," laughed Judith. "But you mustn't do it in front of anyone else. The grand duke wouldn't like being turned into a laughingstock—why, no one would pay him any attention then."

"It's time for bed, dear," announced Marian. Anna climbed up to the loft for the night. But before she fell asleep, she had an idea…

The next week, the Grand Duke Archibald issued yet another decree. As always, he puffed up his chest as he spoke:

"Hear ye, hear ye. Since I grew up with just one mother and one father, and I turned out so well, I proclaim that this arrangement will work best for everyone. In one week any children who have too many mothers or fathers, or not enough, will be thrown into the dungeon."

"He can't do that!" exclaimed Anna softly.

"I'm afraid he can," said Marian, reaching down to hug Anna. "But we'll never let him take you away. We'd flee to another kingdom first."

"Come back next week for another decree," commanded the grand duke. He started to walk off the balcony, then stopped and turned around. "Oh," he added. "In the meantime, don't forget about the jelly beans."

That evening after dinner, Anna had an emergency meeting with her friend Peter. They made a list.

"There's Nicholas," said Anna, "He has two dads. That's one dad too many, according to the grand duke."

"And don't forget his new brother, Jesse."

"And Gaston lives with his grandparents."

"What about Scarlett? And Mia and Joseph."

"And Carmen and James. And—"

Soon they had listed 12 other kids who did not have the right parents, according to the grand duke, and who would be taken away from their families.

The next day, all 12 met secretly in the woods. Anna quickly told them her plan.

The villagers had never seen anything like the week that followed. Children were strutting all about the town, puffing up their chests, holding their noses, and making silly speeches.

"Hear ye, hear ye," said Peter, puffing up his chest and holding his nose as he stood on a park bench. "Henceforth, I proclaim that all pet goldfish must be toilet-trained."

"Hear ye, hear ye," declared Scarlett. "I proclaim that horses are forbidden to burp."

"Hear ye, hear ye," announced Jesse, "I accidentally swallowed a grasshopper when I was 2, and I turned out so well, I proclaim that every 2-year-old must swallow a grasshopper."

Throughout the village, everyone shook their heads and laughed at those silly children.

Everyone, that is, except the Grand Duke Archibald. He knew nothing of all this. He was squirreled away in his castle, studying important papers, and composing his next decree.

On the appointed day, the Grand Duke Archibald again strutted out onto the castle balcony. He looked just like the children as they had strutted about town that week. One or two adults started to laugh as they remembered those silly children, but they stifled themselves quickly. The grand duke did not like people laughing at him!

"Hear ye, hear ye..." announced the grand duke.

But no one was really listening. One woman found herself wondering just how you would toilet-train a goldfish. She tried not to laugh but couldn't help herself. The man next to her thought about burping horses. He too began to laugh. Soon others joined him. They giggled. They chuckled. They laughed so hard their sides hurt. And they couldn't stop. Soon everyone was rolling on the ground, giggling and laughing and chuckling, poking each other and laughing some more.

One man stood up. He held up his nose, puffed out his chest, and announced, "I proclaim that giggling is against the law." Everyone roared with laughter.

"Guards!" roared the Grand Duke Archibald, his face crimson with embarrassment.

"Arrest everyone who's laughing! Off with their heads!"

But the guards were laughing too. "Off with their heads, Off with their noses, Send them to bed, Without any toeses!" sang one guard, and they all laughed some more.

This was too much for the grand duke. He had never been so humiliated in all his life. They were laughing at him!

And so, with his chest still puffed out as far as he could get it, the Grand Duke Archibald strode off the balcony, down the castle stairs, and into his coach. He rode out of the kingdom as fast as he could, and he was never seen or heard from again.

That evening, everyone ate jelly beans for dinner. And except for a few stomachaches that night, they all lived happily every after.

— *The End* —